Lady the dog is very happy in her new home with Jim Dear and his wife, Darling. But when cross Aunt Sara arrives, all that changes! Lady runs away and meets Tramp, a friendly dog who has no home. And then her adventures really begin...

British Library Cataloguing in Publication Data
Walt Disney's Lady and the tramp.
   I. Greene, Ward. Lady and the tramp
   II. Walt Disney Productions
   823'.914[J]   PZ7
   ISBN 0-7214-1021-9

First edition

Published by Ladybird Books Ltd Loughborough Leicestershire UK

Printed in England (7)

$\mathcal{D}$ISNEY

LADY and the TRAMP

Ladybird Books

Jim Dear and his wife Darling lived in a big old house. Darling was lonely during the day when Jim was at work. So, one Christmas, Jim bought Darling a special present.

It was very difficult to keep the present a secret, because it snuffled. It was even more difficult to wrap up, because it wriggled.

It was a little puppy! "She's lovely!" cried Darling. "Let's call her Lady!"

Lady had a lovely Christmas Day.
At bedtime, Jim tucked her up in a
little basket and said, "That's your
very own basket, just for you!"
Then he went upstairs.

But Lady was miserable in her very own basket. So she went upstairs, and found a much better place to sleep – tucked up in Jim's bed!

Lady loved living with Jim Dear
and Darling. Every day she woke
Jim in time for work, and fetched
his slippers. She learned to catch
the newspaper when the boy on his
bicycle threw it to her. She enjoyed

keeping Darling company during the day.

Lady also made friends with two other dogs who lived nearby. One was a bloodhound called Trusty, and the other was a terrier called Jock. Lady was very happy.

But the best part of the day came
when Jim arrived home from work.
After supper, Lady would curl up
for a little snooze, while Jim and
Darling sat by the fire.

One evening, Lady heard Darling

say to Jim, "There are just the three of us now, but it won't be long until the baby makes four!"

Lady didn't know exactly what babies were, but Jim and Darling made them sound fun!

Then, one stormy night, there was great excitement in the house.

A man called Doctor came to see Darling. Soon, Jim was shouting, "It's a boy! It's a boy!" And Lady guessed that the baby had come to make four.

Next morning, Lady was allowed
her first peep at the baby. She was
thrilled! But the baby was very
tiny, and she wondered what it
could do.

She stood up on her back legs to get a better view. Darling said, "When the baby gets bigger, Lady, you'll be able to play with him." Lady wagged her tail. That was just what she'd hoped the baby was for.

One day, Jim got out a box and a bag with labels on them. Darling called this ''luggage'' and she filled the box and bag with clothes. Lady was puzzled.

Then Jim said, ''We're going away for a few days, Lady. Aunt Sara is coming to look after the baby, and you must help with the baby-sitting.'' He patted her, but for some reason Lady felt afraid.

As soon as Aunt Sara arrived, Jim and Darling left in a taxi. Lady felt like crying. She was frightened of Aunt Sara, who seemed very cross.

Lady hid behind the door, and when Aunt Sara was taking her coat off the little dog dashed upstairs. She wanted to guard the baby from this terrible person who had come to live in the house instead of Jim and Darling.

Lady stood up to look in the cot and make sure the baby was still there. But just at that moment Aunt Sara came into the room. She thought Lady was trying to get *into* the baby's cot!

Aunt Sara screamed, and whacked at Lady with her broom. Lady dodged, but Aunt Sara kept whacking away, knocking over tables and everything else that stood in her path. "Get out!" she screamed. "You horrible, bad dog! Get out!"

Lady crept out of the house, her tail drooping and her head bowed. She walked sadly away from home, but had no idea where to go.

Once she got a terrible fright when some fierce dogs bared their teeth at her and growled. She ran and ran, gasping for breath.

At last Lady found a yard behind the railway station where there was no one to shout at her. She flopped down behind a barrel and some old boxes, put her head between her paws, and went to sleep.

Early next morning, a train pulled into the station yard, and out jumped a big, strong dog.

The dog was called Tramp. He had no proper home, but travelled from town to town by riding on trains. Tramp stretched and yawned. "It's a nice day," he said, sleepily. "And this new place looks interesting."

Then he saw Lady hiding behind a barrel. Tramp blinked, and wagged his tail. Lady smiled back shyly. Then Tramp barked. He thought that Lady was beautiful.

Lady felt safe with Tramp. She went exploring with him, and soon they came to a chicken farm. Lady had never seen chickens before, but Tramp had! He dug a hole and wriggled under the fence. Then he bounced right into the middle of the chickens.

Soon, feathers were flying as the chickens tried to get away! When Lady saw what fun Tramp was having, she joined him! Neither of them saw a horse and wagon pulling up alongside the fence.

The driver of the wagon crept up behind the two dogs, and Tramp suddenly realised what was happening. "Run, Lady!" he barked. "It's the man from the dogs' home! Follow me!"

But Lady wasn't quick enough.
The man caught her and threw her
into a cage at the back of his
wagon. Lady found herself
surrounded by strange dogs. She
was being taken away, and Tramp
wasn't there to help her.

Lady was very frightened, but the dogs were friendly and tried to cheer her up. "You'll be safe!" they barked. "You've got a collar, and a tag with your name on it. Don't worry!"

The dogs were right. The next day the man took Lady home. Aunt Sara wasn't pleased to see her. She chained Lady up outside and yelled, "Stay there! Don't you make any noise, or I'll send you back to that dogs' home!"

Lady was too miserable to sleep.
She gave a little bark of misery,
and a sad little howl, but very
quietly so that Aunt Sara wouldn't
hear. Then she stiffened. What
was that rustling in the leaves?
Something was running up the
steps to the house. It was a rat!
And it was heading for the door.

Lady pulled and tugged at her
chain, and just as it snapped there
was a low *"Woof!"* Tramp had
been searching for Lady, and had
heard her sad little bark.

Lady was so pleased to see him.

She told him all about the rat.
Together they raced into the house
and up the stairs. They found the
rat in the baby's room! It ran
under a table, but Tramp knew
exactly what to do.

Tramp fought with the rat and the terrible noise reached Aunt Sara's room. She came rushing in and whacked Tramp with her broom,

chasing him into a cupboard. Then she turned to deal with Lady.

Just as Aunt Sara lifted her broom to hit poor Lady, there was a voice downstairs calling, "Hell-oooo! Anybody home?" It was Jim Dear! Lady almost swooned with happiness!

Aunt Sara went rushing down to Jim and Darling. "I've just found a horrible dog in the baby's room!" she cried. "And that dog of yours was no help at all!"

But Lady took no notice of Aunt Sara. She barked at Jim Dear, and jumped up and down, then ran back and forth to the stairs. "She's trying to tell us something!" said Darling.

Lady led them all to the nursery, and showed them the dead rat.

She ran over to the cupboard where Tramp was shut in, and barked, her tail wagging. Jim Dear suddenly realised what she was telling them. "The mongrel was helping Lady to protect our baby!" he cried.

They opened the cupboard, and Tramp crept out expecting to be beaten. "Good dog!" said Jim, and Tramp looked up in surprise. No one had ever spoken kindly to him before. "You must stay with us for ever!" he heard the kind voice say, and slowly Tramp began to wag his tail. Lady was delighted.

Tramp soon became one of the family, and that made five. He made friends with Trusty and Jock, too, and was so big and strong that bully dogs never dared to come near them!

Soon it was Christmas again, but this time the best presents of all were... well... one of them looked like Tramp and the others looked like Lady! But Jim, Darling, the baby, and Lady and the Tramp all thought that the puppies were wonderful! And together they made six... seven... eight...